DAVID N. CHURCH P. S.
230 JAMES STREET
ORILLIA, ONT.   L3V 1M2

DISCARDED

HOUSE CALLS

House Calls

THE TRUE STORY OF A
PIONEER DOCTOR

AINSLIE MANSON

ILLUSTRATIONS BY
Mary Jane Gerber

A GROUNDWOOD BOOK
DOUGLAS & McINTYRE
VANCOUVER TORONTO BUFFALO

In memory of my great-great-grandfather, Dr. John Hutchison, and my great-grandfather, Ralph Burton Hutchison, the first child born in the Bonfire House. And for all the Hutchison family descendants. — A M

To Dr. O'Toole, with love. — M J G

ACKNOWLEDGMENTS

Kathleen, the fictitious protagonist of this story, is a compilation of many different people. I have taken the liberty of conveniently placing her cottage within view of the Bonfire House.

I would like to acknowledge the help and assistance of the staff and volunteers of Hutchison House Museum, members of the Peterborough Historical Society, Heather Blyth and Dr. Jackie Duffin at the Museum of Health Care for Eastern Ontario, Ernst Stieb at The Niagara Apothecary, Lee Perry at the Medical Library of the University of British Columbia, and Dr. Nancy Turner, ethnobotanist at the University of Victoria. Also special thanks to helpful cousins and descendants of Dr. Hutchison — David Bate, Peggy Oliver Sarjeant and Lindsay Stewart Morgan — and to my personal in-house medical authority, David Manson. — A M

Thanks to the historical interpreters at Black Creek Pioneer Village, especially Robin Baker for her carriage-and-harness demonstrations. Thanks also to the people at Hutchison House for their tour and assistance. — M J G

Text copyright © 2001 by Ainslie Manson
Illustrations copyright © 2001 by Mary Jane Gerber

All rights reserved. No part of this book may be reproduced, stored in a retrieval system or transmitted in any form or by any means, without the prior written permission of the publisher or, in the case of photocopying or other reprographic copying, a licence from CANCOPY (Canadian Reprography Collective), Toronto, Ontario.

Groundwood Books / Douglas & McIntyre
720 Bathurst Street, Suite 400,
Toronto, Ontario M5S 2R4

Distributed in the USA by Publishers Group West
1700 Fourth Street, Berkeley, CA 94710

We acknowledge the financial support of the Canada Council for the Arts, the Ontario Arts Council and the Government of Canada through the Book Publishing Industry Development Program for our publishing activities.

ONTARIO ARTS COUNCIL
CONSEIL DES ARTS DE L'ONTARIO

National Library of Canada
Cataloguing in Publication Data
Manson, Ainslie
House calls : the true story of a pioneer doctor
"A Groundwood book".
Includes bibliographical references.
ISBN 0-88899-446-X
1. Hutchison, John, d. 1847 — Juvenile literature. 2. Medicine — Canada — History — 19th century — Juvenile literature. I. Gerber, Mary Jane. II. Title.
R464.H872M36 2001   j610'.92   C2001-930644-X

Printed and bound in Canada

CONTENTS

ONE · DR. HUTCHISON · 7
Consumption · 9 *Amputation* · 13

TWO · THE BACKWOODS · 15
Leeches · 19 *Wash Your Hands!* · 20 *Ague* · 24

THREE · HOUSE PARTY · 27
Sisters Writing in the Wilderness · 30

FOUR · DISTURBING NEWS · 35
Kathleen's Scones · 36 *Women and Medicine* · 38
First Woman Doctor? · 42

FIVE · THE BONFIRE HOUSE · 45
The Keeping Room · 48 *Childbirth* · 50

EPILOGUE · 52

GLOSSARY · 54

FOR FURTHER INFORMATION · 55

ONE
Dr. Hutchison

"Here he comes!" I called to Mama. "Dr. Hutchison is coming!"

He came striding up our garden path. A little breeze made dappled, dancing shadows in the sunshine, and it looked as though the daffodils were waving and bowing to him.

Though Dr. H. had declared that I was now almost fit as a fiddle, he still came to our house quite regularly. On doctor days I'd rest my elbows on the windowsill, waiting and watching for him.

"You should be outside, Kathleen," he called. "Fresh air is what you need now. Fresh air and exercise."

I laughed. He always greeted me this way.

"I've not forgotten," I assured him.

I hurried to the door. We bowed to one another and I pretended to look solemn as he handed me his doctor's case.

"Will you assist me this morning, Kathleen?"

I nodded. I loved pretending I was a real doctor. I led him to the keeping room where Mama was waiting. I walked carefully, because I knew that behind me, Dr. H. was making sure that my back was straight and that I was not leaning or limping.

I placed his case on the kitchen table. Dr. H. always let me take things out for him as he needed them.

THE DOCTOR'S BAG

In Dr. Hutchison's day, the doctor's "black bag" was often a boxlike chest or case. It contained the few instruments and supplies used by a nineteenth-century country doctor.

lancet case	blood-collecting
tooth forceps	bowl
whiskey and opium	obstetric forceps
bandages	plasters and
scissors	poultices
medicines	stethoscope
tourniquet	

He boosted me up onto the table. He tapped my chest, then held out his hand.

"Stethoscope, please, Kathleen."

There had been no stethoscope when I first had consumption. In those days Dr. Hutchison listened to my chest and to my father's chest with just his ear or a paper cone.

Papa had had consumption like me, only his illness had been far more serious. He had galloping consumption, and it was fast and fatal. Dr. Hutchison and my papa were close friends. Before Papa died, Dr. H. promised him that he would make me well again.

"Stay still, Kathleen." Dr. H. was listening to my chest. First I had to be as quiet as a mouse, and then he wanted to hear my voice through the wall of my chest. "Now speak, Kathleen!"

I couldn't think what to say, so I quoted a line from a poem by John Gay: "*Is there no hope? The sick man said; The silent doctor shook his head.*"

Dr. H. laughed as he examined my arms and legs and moved them in all directions.

"Now open up, Kathleen!" He looked far down my throat. "Turn your head a little more toward the light. Ah, that's better."

I tried to imagine what it would

CONSUMPTION

In the early 1800s, tuberculosis (TB) was known as consumption. Though primarily a lung disease, TB can affect many different parts of the body, including the bones. The disease spread rapidly in large families, where often more than one person slept in each bed. Convalescence was long, and many children remained crippled for life.

In Dr. Hutchison's day, little was known about how to treat consumption. Doctors were beginning to realize, however, that nutritious food and complete bed rest did help in the early stages of the disease. If patients began to regain their strength, they were urged to get lots of fresh air and exercise.

During the eighteenth and nineteenth centuries, more than one billion people died of consumption. Some believed the disease would eventually result in the end of civilization. In the late 1800s, sanitariums were built to treat patients with long-term bed rest, fresh air and light exercise. Though sanitarium stays could last for years, many lives were saved, partly because the disease did not spread so readily.

Today, doctors can control tuberculosis with vaccines and modern drugs, though these are not always affordable or available. Every minute, one person still dies of TB somewhere in the world.

be like to have Dr. H. as my father. Then I remembered his five sons. I didn't think I would like to have William, James, John, Henry and George as brothers, even though each Sunday I did enjoy trying to guess what they were going to do next in church. They would burst through the door, pushing and shoving one another. They were usually in trouble even before they got to their seats! Poor Mrs. Hutchison generally had to cope with them on her own, as Dr. H. was regularly called off on emergencies.

"Kathleen?" Mama's voice interrupted my thoughts. "Are you wool gathering? Dr. Hutchison has just issued us an invitation…"

I thought how fortunate it was that he couldn't read my thoughts the way he could read my bones!

"Mrs. Hutchison and I wondered if you and your mother would like to come for noon-day dinner on Friday," he said. "Do you think you're strong enough to face my horde?"

"Oh, yes!" I jumped down from the table to demonstrate my strength.

When I was first ill, Dr. Hutchison confined me to my bed for several months. Then, as I improved, he slowly introduced me to his fresh air and exercise regime. At first I had to lean on Mama, and I could only walk as far as the pond, where we would rest a little and perhaps look for tadpoles. As I grew stronger, our walks grew longer. We'd go into the woods to admire the carpets of white trumpety trilliums in the spring or the blazing red maple trees in the autumn.

Eventually I could walk all the way to the village to fetch things for Mama from the shops, or up the hill to the new stone church. I still had to stop and catch my breath on hills, but I could tell I was getting better.

And now Dr. H. thought I was ready for a luncheon party with his family! My heart felt light as I watched him stride off down the road, swinging the twisted thorn walking staff that he always carried.

I could hardly wait till Friday.

❧

I had always wanted to see inside the Hutchisons' house. The outside was barely visible from the road, but I was sure it would be enormous, since Dr. H. had such a large family. I also expected it would be quite grand. After all, he was doctor to a great many people.

Instead, Mrs. Hutchison greeted us at the door of the smallest cottage imaginable. It was like a doll's house, but the Hutchison boys were not dolls. We could hear them hollering even before they threw open the door. They fell over one another trying to be first to greet

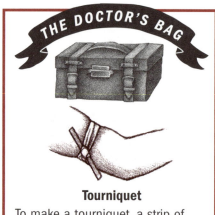

Tourniquet
To make a tourniquet, a strip of cloth was wrapped around a limb and twisted tight to stop the flow of blood.

us, and they pushed and shoved so furiously that they almost knocked Mama off the stoop.

"Manners, boys!" their mother commanded, but I don't think they heard her.

William and Dr. Hutchison seemed to be missing. Only seconds later, however, William flew into the room by swinging down from the loft on a rope! I looked up nervously, wondering whether Dr. H. would make his entrance in the same manner.

The cottage was so small I felt as though we all had to turn at the same time. We were like spoons in a drawer! After our meal, little George went to his cot for a nap, and the rest of us were sent outside. I sank down thankfully on the front step. James, John and Henry tore off down the road, but William came and sat beside me.

"Where's your papa?" I asked.

"Tending to emergencies as usual," said William. "I expect right about now he's sawing off one of Caleb Clark's legs." He plucked a blade of grass and stuck the stem in his mouth. "Poor old fellow was trying to get his wagon out of a mire, and the oxen pulled the wagon

AMPUTATION

In the 1800s, when an arm or leg was badly damaged (with bone protruding through an open wound), doctors often had to amputate. Otherwise, severe infection (gangrene) could set in and spread to the rest of the body, resulting in certain death. The patient was generally awake through the whole procedure and simply had to be brave.

Doctors learned to be resourceful. Dr. Pitkin Gross (1791-1873) was once called upon to amputate a leg in backwoods Ontario. He was far from the nearest community and did not even have his doctor's bag with him. Without hesitation, he sharpened and reshaped the blade of a sickle on a grindstone. Then he bound the leg with a tourniquet and quickly cut it off while neighbors held the patient down. The patient recovered.

When it came to amputations, time was of the utmost importance. The skill of the surgeon was judged largely by his speed and the small amount of blood on his frock coat.

"In the first place, you must not divide the skin by scratches. You must carry the knife completely through the tissues at once, and doing it with rapidity you will save the patient a great deal of pain." —SURGEON'S INSTRUCTION MANUAL IN THE 1830S

> **THE MEDICINE GARDEN**
> *Early settlers often grew or collected plants to use as medicines. They brought some of their plant knowledge from their home countries but also learned about the value of local plants from the native people. The settlers made healing teas and infusions by steeping leaves or petals in boiling water. They crushed leaves to make poultices or combined leaves with animal fat to make ointments. Roots and bark were ground up to make powdered medicines. Many of these early remedies had a sound medicinal basis and are still used today.*

right over him. Mud, blood and shattered bones. Father has been trying to save his legs, but the infection spread like wildfire so I doubt he was able to." He looked up at the sound of a horse's hooves. "Here he comes now. Kathleen, you might want to hide your eyes. He'll be dripping with blood."

"I don't mind blood at all," I said.

"Oh," said William, looking a little disappointed. The buggy stopped by the cottage door. There was no sign of blood, and Dr. H. looked quite cheerful.

"I've a few more calls to make out in the country," he announced. "Would you two like to come with me?"

I sprang to my feet, tripping on my skirt and catching my balance by using William's head as a knoll post.

"Oh, yes, please!"

Mama agreed and came out to wave us on our way. William gave Molly a feed of oats and then helped me into the buggy.

"We'll no doubt dine with the Stewarts and be back quite late," Dr. H. said as he gently tapped Molly with a rein to start her off. "Don't you worry, Margaret. We'll take good care of Kathleen."

TWO
The Backwoods

The countryside unfolded before us. In the woods, deer sprang away as we trotted by. We waved to farmers working in their fields and they waved back. The air was filled with birdsong, and we breathed in the scents of all the different wildflowers.

"First stop, the Wrights' farm," said Dr. Hutchison, turning down a grassy lane.

"We were just about to have a cup of tea," said Mrs. Wright, coming out onto her verandah to greet us.

She produced a pound cake, hot from the oven, and freshly baked bread with strawberry jam. William and Simon Wright competed to see who could eat the most the fastest. Simon had a broken arm, but it didn't seem to slow him down.

"How did you break your arm?" I asked.

"Abigail," Simon replied.

"Abigail is our milking cow," Mr. Wright explained. "Simon forgot about her sore hip. He tried to shove her over so he could get into the stall to milk her. Abigail wouldn't have it. She slammed him against the wall and then when Simon fell, that crack-brained cow trod on him."

Simon scowled. "She's a mean old grouch," he said, continuing to stuff cake into his mouth.

"We should get rid of the ill-tempered beast," said Mrs. Wright.

"Edith, you know we can't afford to," said Mr. Wright. "Where would we get another cow?"

Dr. H. sprang to his feet.

"Right," he said. "Thank you for the tea, but now we must get on with it. Kathleen, could you assist me, please?"

I handed him the surgical scissors. He cocked his head to one side and eyed the ragged bandages on Simon's arm.

"No question about it," he said, pointing to the arm. "That has to come off!"

Simon's face turned green, and I thought he was going to lose

THE MEDICINE GARDEN
Comfrey: Ointment and tea made from the roots and leaves were used to help heal broken bones, reduce bruising and relieve burns.

more than just his appetite! We all quickly assured him that it was the bandage that was coming off and not the arm.

As Dr. H. snipped off the old dressing, he explained how I should make a padding to go under the splint. Mrs. Wright supplied lovely soft material that had once been a flannel nightgown. To hold the splint in place we used strips of worn but well-washed old shirts.

We were then ready to leave, but the Wrights insisted that we have one more cup of tea. As we sipped, they pressed us for news of their friends and acquaintances.

I was just beginning to wonder how many more calls we had to make when Dr. Hutchison caught my eye, and we rose to our feet. As we worked our way to the buggy, Mrs. Wright handed me a letter for her friend Mrs. Taylor.

"Our doctor is always happy to act as postman," she explained.

Mr. Wright turned to William. "If you're going to the Stewarts, could you return a chisel for me?"

"Certainly," said William. Mr. Wright then handed him not only the chisel but also two chickens and a cured ham.

"For your father," he said quietly.

We thanked and were thanked. We nodded and smiled and thanked again. I thought we might be there until the sun set, but we finally waved our farewells and moved on.

Now the farms were farther apart, and though the forest was

being cleared away, most fields were still covered with stumps. On the corduroy road, where logs had been laid across our path for long stretches, I had to hold on to the seat with both hands.

As soon as the buggy came to a stop, William raced off to see young Tom, who was clearing a field with his father.

I was surprised at how unfinished the Taylors' cabin was. I could see daylight through some of the cracks between the logs. There was no glass in the windows and no room partitions. The dirt floor looked quite damp in places. I thought how cold the cabin must be in the winter.

Our first patient was Mrs. Taylor's elderly father. The old man was not actually ill, but like many of Dr. H.'s patients, he was a firm believer in being bled at least once a year. He looked on cheerfully as I removed the correct lancet from the case and laid it beside the bleeding bowl on the table.

I cringed a little when Dr. Hutchison made a small incision in Grampa Goodfellow's arm, but the old man simply smiled a wide, toothless smile.

"Don't be afraid to let it run," he said happily as he watched his blood drip into the bowl. "It's been a long while since I've been bled and it does me good, I know it does."

But Dr. H. stopped up the incision with a small bandage when he had about a teacup full. I helped Grampa Goodfellow to a bed in the corner and covered him with a blanket. Then Dr. H. was on to his next patient.

Five-year-old Cecelia also had to be bled. She had an infection in her right arm. It was sore and swollen, and she had been running a fever for several days.

THE MEDICINE GARDEN
Yarrow: Tea made from the dried flowers eased headaches and colds and relieved the pain of angina. The whole plant was applied to help heal cuts and burns.

When bleeding children, Dr. H. generally used leeches instead of a lancet.

Cecelia was not at all happy with the prospect, and I could feel my own tummy churning. But I was determined to demonstrate that I was an able assistant. I made Cecelia's small corn husk doll dance across her pillow.

"Look, Cecelia, look!" I said, trying to keep her attention.

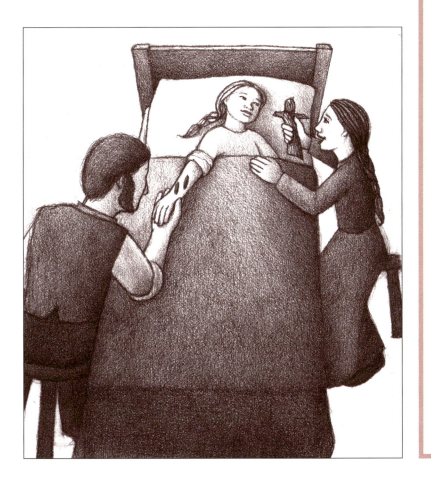

LEECHES

A leech is a type of worm (nematode) with a sucker at each end of its body. Also called bloodsuckers, leeches were used to reduce inflammation (swelling).

If the doctor wanted to remove a leech before it was full of blood, he could sprinkle it with salt, and the leech would shrivel and drop off. Some leeches were kept in a jar and used many times.

At one time the word leech meant to cure or heal. Doctors were sometimes called leechers, and the practice of medicine was known as leechery.

"There is one objection...to the use of leeches in children, which deserves attention," wrote Dr. Clutterbuck in a medical paper from London in 1840, *"namely, the terror they sometimes occasion, with a continuance of angry feelings for an hour or two, while the operation lasts."*

WASH YOUR HANDS!

One hundred and fifty years ago, people were just beginning to understand that living in squalid conditions or close to smelly garbage or stagnant water could cause illness. No one understood the concept of spreading germs, but people did realize that cleanliness somehow helped prevent illness. Dr. Hutchison would not have sterilized his instruments, but he would have washed them with soap and warm water.

Today the need for sterilization is far more clearly understood, but signs are still posted in many hospitals reminding workers to wash their hands frequently.

On the other side of the bed, Dr. H. placed a spot of milk on her upper arm where he wanted the leech to suck, then slid the leech down a leech-tube to that spot. When it had attached itself, he applied a few more in the same manner. I made the doll sing and dance faster and faster. Cecelia began to laugh.

Grampa Goodfellow was on his feet again by this time, so we brought a chair to Cecelia's bedside, and the old man said he would sit by her and keep her happy until the leeches grew fat and dropped off.

The Taylor farm was at a crossroads, and it was one of the places where Dr. H. always checked for

Tooth Forceps
In Dr. Hutchison's day, there were no sophisticated drills or other dental equipment. Badly decayed teeth were simply pulled out using special tongs.

messages. Mrs. Taylor passed on a message from the Simpson family. They were new to the area and apparently very much in need of a doctor.

Mrs. Taylor pushed a large earthenware crock across the table to me.

"Kathleen, this is soup," she said. "Do you think you could balance it on your lap as far as the Simpsons?"

She walked with us to the buggy, a basket on her arm. She tucked the basket into the buggy by Dr. H.'s feet.

"That's for you," she said. "I wish it was more."

As soon as we were out of sight, William leaned across me and peered into the basket.

"There's oatcakes, and maple syrup, and potato bread and a dozen eggs. You'll notice, Kathleen, that Father never says no to these tasty tidbits. If this goes on much longer, he'll grow so plump, the buggy will collapse!"

THE MEDICINE GARDEN
Lemon balm: Tea made from the leaves soothed tension, headaches and toothaches.

I gave Dr. Hutchison a quick sideways glance. There wasn't an ounce of fat on him!

The road became worse and worse. It was hard to keep the soup steady on my knee. The corduroy road had been smooth compared to the deep ruts we now encountered. Eventually we sighted a cabin through the trees ahead of us, but the road was a sea of mud.

"William, you stay here with Molly. Let her eat a little grass," Dr. H. said. "Kathleen, you come with me and bring that soup."

He lifted me across the mud to the side of the road, and then William handed down the soup crock.

The cabin was in a state of collapse. It looked as if it was about to be swallowed up by the forest around it.

"Are we in the right place?" I asked as we came closer. "It looks deserted."

"The Taylors mentioned the old cabin," said Dr. H. "I think the Simpson family is just living in it until they can get their own completed."

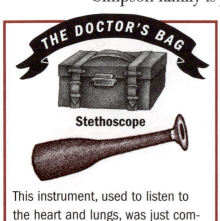

THE DOCTOR'S BAG
Stethoscope
This instrument, used to listen to the heart and lungs, was just coming into use in North America during Dr. Hutchison's time.

When we knocked, someone called out. Dr. H. stooped to enter the low doorway and I followed.

It was cold and dark inside. There was just one small window. I noticed a fireplace, but there was no fire in the hearth.

I pulled my shawl tightly around my shoulders. The room smelled foul, and I found it hard to breathe.

There was a table in the middle of the room. It was piled high with dishes and pots, and the air was thick with flies and buzzing mosquitoes.

I became aware of a sound other than the buzzing. It was almost like the mewing of a kitten.

Something was crawling toward us. I gasped. It was a small child!

As I bent down to pick up the baby, Dr. Hutchison stopped me with an outstretched arm.

"I'll tend to this alone, Kathleen." My eyes had become more used to the dim light, and as he guided me back to the door, I saw the disheveled, crowded bed in the corner. Every member of the family except the baby must have been in that one small bed.

"You and William tether Molly, gather some wood and stack it by the door," Dr. H. instructed in a low voice. "Bring in the baskets from the Wrights and Taylors as well. I think the need here is greater than ours."

I took big gulps of clean, fresh air as I hurried back to the buggy. While we gathered the wood, William and I discovered the beginnings of a log house behind the ramshackle cabin. It was close to a small

AGUE

Many early settlers suffered from ague (pronounced AY-gyoo), or swamp fever. Victims developed chills so severe their teeth would chatter. Then they would burn up with high fevers. Shortly after Dr. Hutchison's death, the drug quinine became available as a remedy and was a great help to sufferers.

Ague was actually a malarial infection, and it ran rampant not only in Ontario but also in parts of the eastern and southern United States until the second half of the nineteenth century. A mosquito that bred in swamps and open stagnant water spread the infection. As land was cleared and these wet areas began to disappear, so did the disease.

lake, in a lovely location, but so far the walls came only up to our knees.

We had stacked a fairly good-sized pile of wood by the time Dr. H. reappeared.

"Is the whole family very ill?" I asked when we were underway.

"They're having a bad time of it," he replied. "They all have ague, even the baby. At first I thought it might be typhoid fever or even cholera. That's why I didn't want you in there, Kathleen."

I couldn't imagine being so sick and living so far from my neighbors.

"Will they get better?" I asked.

"Oh, yes," Dr. H. reassured me. "But ague is so utterly debilitating when it strikes. When the whole family gets sick at the same time, there's no one to cook or farm or look after the children."

I tried to look through the forest as we wended our way back along the muddy road. I felt I should be able to see light in the distance, but the blackness went on and on. Then the forest thinned a little, and we could see a river. The sun was sparkling on the water. I was happy to see the sky again.

We passed a turning, and I could see an Indian village through the trees. Three Indian children — two girls and a boy — were standing by the side of the road. When they recognized the buggy, they ran along beside us, calling out to Dr. Hutchison.

THE MEDICINE GARDEN
Arnica: The flower heads were applied to sprains, bruises and burns.

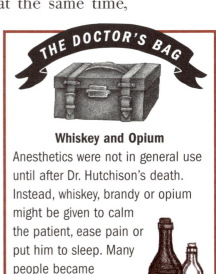

Whiskey and Opium
Anesthetics were not in general use until after Dr. Hutchison's death. Instead, whiskey, brandy or opium might be given to calm the patient, ease pain or put him to sleep. Many people became addicted to opium if they took it for too long.

"They're patients of mine," he said, as he pulled Molly to a stop and greeted each of them by name.

The older girl held up a basket of small plants for Dr. H. to admire. She was about my age. Her shiny black hair came almost to her waist. When she realized I was looking at her, she looked down, embarrassed. I felt embarrassed, too, and was sorry I had stared.

"Bunchberry, right?" said Dr. H., examining the green leaves. The children nodded approvingly. It was as though he was their pupil, and he'd passed a test.

"They use it as medicine," he explained to William and me. "In this village they make a tea from the leaves to ease colds or reduce fevers."

The older girl reached into the buggy and handed me one perfect plant bearing an early flower. I nodded my thanks and wished I had something to give her in return. I twirled the stem between my fingers as Dr. H. clicked gently to start Molly on her way.

THREE
House Party

"Whoa, Molly." Dr. H. reined in. We had come to a river, but the water was so high that it lapped over the boards of the wooden bridge ahead of us. "We'll lead Molly across." He shouted to be heard over the thundering river.

"Father, isn't this where you once swam the river when you were going to the Stewarts?"

Dr. H. pointed back the way we had come. "It was by the Indian village. Before they built this bridge, I used to leave Molly there. Usually they would take me across in a canoe, but that day there were none. Still, I had to get across. The Stewarts had a very sick child and they were waiting for me. Since it was autumn, the river was much lower than it is today. I thought I could wade across, but at about the halfway mark I was swept off my feet and carried downstream."

"He kept his medical case dry, though," William added as he helped me down from the buggy. "He held it up above his head!"

"The case stayed dry," said Dr. Hutchison, "but I certainly didn't!"

William chuckled. "Then Father spent two nights lost in the forest!"

"Gracious!" I said. "That doesn't sound like a laughing matter!"

"You're quite right, Kathleen. The poor Stewarts were as anxious about me as they were about their child, and my own family couldn't think what on earth had become of me."

"Couldn't you have just walked back along the riverbank?" William asked.

"I tried, but there were too many obstacles. Trees down, cliffs… and then it got dark."

"How did you get dry?" I asked. "How did you stay warm?"

"I got quite dry just walking. Then when I knew I was truly lost, I lit a fire. Fortunately I had a flint with me," he said, gathering Molly's reins and raising her head. "Come on, old girl, not far now."

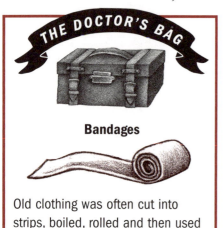

Bandages

Old clothing was often cut into strips, boiled, rolled and then used and reused as bandages.

I watched from the solid shore as he led Molly onto the slippery bridge. I wondered whether I would have been brave enough to wade the river to get to a patient. William took my hand and we followed. The water lapped against the logs. I didn't look down.

"Getting to the Stewarts is always an adventure," William said as we climbed back into the buggy. "But not half as exciting as being there. I wonder what sort of emergencies we'll have to deal with today?"

"This time we'll just be returning a chisel and paying a social call," said Dr. H. "You never know, though. They do seem to have their disasters!"

"Father has performed many an amputation on their kitchen table," said William nonchalantly. "It's usually pretty gruesome. Once one of the Stewarts passed out right on the table and didn't know what was happening until he woke up…without his head!"

I imagined a Stewart boy running around without a head, like a chicken being prepared for the stewing pot.

"William, what nonsense!" said Dr. H. "Stop trying to scare Kathleen!"

The Stewart household was a lively one. They had four daughters and six sons and there seemed to be no end of extras, as well.

We were invited to share their evening meal. To add to the occasion, Mr. and Mrs. Traill arrived with their new baby just before we sat down. Their older children had been staying with the Stewarts and now, since Mr. Traill was going to be away, Mrs. Traill and the baby were coming to stay for a few days.

SISTERS WRITING IN THE WILDERNESS

Catharine Parr Traill and Susanna Moodie came to Canada from England in 1832. The sisters were both writers.

The Traills were patients of Dr. Hutchison's, and he delivered five of their children.

A short story, or sketch, entitled "The Old Doctor" was discovered in one of Catharine Parr Traill's journals after she died. It is a little-disguised portrait of Dr. Hutchison ("a model of strength, both mental and physical") and gives us a delightful picture of some of the doctor's medical beliefs, including his firm disapproval of overheated bedrooms.

I do not object to an open fireplace, or a hall stove if there must be a stove at all to take off the keen edge of the frosty air, but no bedroom stove at all. I never sleep in a hot room—neither allow one for my children... — CATHARINE PARR TRAILL, "THE OLD DOCTOR"

I could have talked to Mrs. Traill all night. There were so many questions I wanted to ask her! I knew she was a writer but hadn't realized that she wrote children's books as well as books for grown-ups.

Since Mr. Stewart was not at home, Dr. H. was asked to carve the turkey.

"Would you like a leg, Kathleen?" he asked.

"Just like I said," William chortled, giving me a nudge. "Amputations on the kitchen table!"

But there were no emergencies of any kind that evening. After dinner the boys put extra logs in the large open fireplace in the parlor. Then one of them produced a fiddle and one of the older girls sat down at the piano. Mrs. Stewart told me how it had been transported

32 *House Calls*

up the frozen river in the wintertime, and how they had nearly lost it through the ice.

Despite all the music and activity, I noticed that Dr. H. was sound asleep sitting bolt upright in a wingback chair.

"He delivered a baby last night," William explained. "He never got to bed."

"Fortunately our good doctor has always been able to fall asleep anywhere," said Mrs. Stewart. "We'll leave him be, and just dance around him."

We truly did dance around him. I joined in, too. I wanted the evening to go on forever, but of course Dr. H. woke up and noticed the time.

A few of the Stewarts walked back with us as far as the bridge and saw us safely across. When we were underway, the motion of the wagon lulled me to sleep. I dreamed I was a doctor, off on my country rounds, patching wounds and applying poultices.

When I woke up I couldn't see the road at all, just a pathway of thousands of stars in the sky above us.

"How does Molly know where to go?" I whispered to Dr. H., not wanting to wake William, who had fallen asleep as well.

"Instinct," Dr. H. replied. "I just give her a loose rein and even in the worst winter blizzards, she gets me home safely."

THE MEDICINE GARDEN
Horseradish: A poultice of grated root eased stings and reduced inflammation. A paste made from the root was massaged into sore, stiff limbs.

FOUR
Disturbing News

Our house seemed extra quiet after visiting with the Hutchisons and the Stewarts. Mama and I chatted to one another, and we worked on my lessons. We even read aloud most evenings, but it simply wasn't the same.

Dr. Hutchison came by again just a few days later. It seemed a little soon, but we were always glad to see him.

He began in the usual fashion by examining each of my limbs.

"No ill effects from our late night out?" He was using his stethoscope to listen to my chest and I was supposed to be silent, so I just shook my head.

"Good, good," he said somewhat absentmindedly. Then he added abruptly, "Up and be doing now." And the examination was over.

I thought he must be rushing off somewhere on an emergency, but he accepted Mama's invitation to stay for tea. She set up the tray and I put out the scones I had just finished baking.

"You will make someone a fine wife some day, Kathleen," he said when he had taken his first bite.

I considered telling him right then about my plan to become a doctor. I wondered, though, if it might be wiser to wait until I was older and braver. I knew he felt strongly that a woman's place was in the home.

KATHLEEN'S SCONES

At Hutchison House Museum in the summer time, afternoon tea is served in the garden. The servers are young women dressed in nineteenth-century costume, and the scones they serve are very similar to these.

2 cups (500 mL) all-purpose flour
1/3 cup (75 mL) granulated sugar
4 tsp (20 mL) baking powder
1/2 tsp (2 mL) salt
1/3 cup (75 mL) butter or margarine
1/2 cup (125 mL) currants or raisins
1 egg
3/4 cup (175 mL) milk

In a large bowl, combine the flour, sugar, baking powder and salt. Using clean hands, rub in the butter until the mixture resembles coarse crumbs. Add the currants.

In a separate bowl, beat the egg. Add the milk and beat well. Add to the dry ingredients all at once and mix until the dough is moistened. Add a little extra flour if the dough is very sticky.

Flour your hands and then toss the dough lightly on a floured surface. Divide the dough into three portions. Pat or roll each piece into a circle about 1/2 inch (1 cm) thick and cut each circle into four pie-shaped pieces.

Place the pieces on an oiled baking sheet and bake at 400 F (200 C) until golden brown, about 15 minutes.

As I pondered, I heard him clear his throat. I glanced up and was disturbed by his troubled expression.

"I have some…rather sad news," he said. "I am going to have to leave Peterborough."

My teacup slipped from my hand and shattered on the floor. I expected a scolding, but Mama didn't even notice.

"Why?" she whispered.

"It's the boys," said Dr. H. somewhat desperately. "You see, they won't stop growing!"

In spite of our shock, Mama and I burst out laughing.

"Boys do have a way of growing," said Mama with a sad smile. "But you can't move away from it, John. They do it everywhere, not just in Peterborough."

"I know, I know," he said. "But you see, we don't fit in the cottage anymore! We're bursting at the seams!"

"Couldn't you just find a bigger house?" I asked.

"I've tried," he said sadly. "But there are none. And even though I own a piece of land, I have no money for house building."

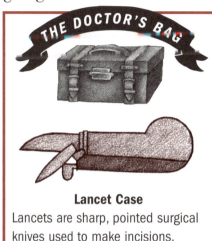

Lancet Case
Lancets are sharp, pointed surgical knives used to make incisions.

WOMEN AND MEDICINE

Women have always been accepted as comforting healers, but it was not until the mid 1800s that they were finally allowed to become licenced medical doctors, and not without an incredible struggle.

In 1849, Elizabeth Blackwell was finally accepted into a small medical school in upstate New York. Many men were opposed to this decision, but she was so hardworking, so courteous and dignified, that she eventually won everyone over. And when she graduated, she topped her class.

In Canada, the struggle went on even longer. In 1863, when Emily Howard Jennings Stowe applied for admission to medical school, she was told that female students would be disruptive and bad for discipline. It was felt that women couldn't possibly cope with medicine — it was far too difficult! Emily decided to go to the U.S. for her training. But when she returned to Ontario, she was refused a license because she hadn't attended a Canadian medical school.

Emily Stowe and Jeannie Trout were finally permitted to attend medical school lectures in Toronto in 1870. Before entering a classroom, they had to peek through a peephole to make sure the room was clear of any embarrassing material. This was to accommodate their sensitivities!

I knew that Dr. H. was paid three dollars a year by each of his patient families. I wondered why he couldn't use that money.

He seemed to read my mind.

"Most families are unable to pay for my services with real money. They simply don't have any. Instead they give me a chicken, a lamb or baskets of vegetables. Or they shovel snow for us in the winter or turn over our vegetable plot in the spring. We appreciate all their help, but unfortunately one cannot pay for house building with a basket of potatoes or a well-dug garden."

"Oh, John, you can't leave!" said Mama desperately. "My Kath is alive because of you. And she's just one of your many grateful patients."

That afternoon I watched Dr. Hutchison walk slowly back down our garden path. He wasn't swinging his staff the way he usually did. He was leaning on it.

THE MEDICINE GARDEN
Dandelion: *A tea made from the leaves helped digestion and eased rheumatism. Juice from the roots relieved stiff, sore joints.*

The news spread from neighbor to neighbor, and soon everyone knew that Dr. Hutchison was planning to leave.

"We can't let this happen!" said one neighbor.

"You're right, we can't," said another. "He's our friend, not just our doctor."

I was amazed to discover how many people depended on Dr. H. He was not only a family doctor, he was an army surgeon as well, attending to the needs of all army personnel in and near Peterborough. He was doctor for the Indian village we had passed on the way to the Stewarts, he was coroner for our district, and he even served as a justice of the peace.

For a few weeks everyone simply moped and looked miserable.

Then it was as though a few of their doctor's own words began to ring in their ears.

"God helps those who help themselves!" they said. "Up and be doing, up and be doing!"

A town meeting was called. It was held in the church on the hill. I sat at the back with a few other children.

"We can't lure him with promises of higher wages," said a lady with a thick Scottish burr.

"No," said a man with a gravely voice. "Few of us pay him with real money as it is."

"And besides," said my mother, "what the Hutchisons really need is a larger house."

"And there are no houses of any size available at the moment," said a man in the back row. "Our community is growing too fast."

"But as I recall, John Hutchison does own a piece of land…" said one man thoughtfully. "Possibly he could build there…"

"You're forgetting that he has no money for house building. Land or no land."

It seemed there was no solution.

The meeting was about to close when I found myself rising to my feet.

"I have an idea," I said. My voice sounded small and shaky. Everyone turned and stared.

"Maybe," I continued slowly, "we could build him a house?"

Someone laughed. "And who would *we* be?" he asked sarcastically.

"Why…all his patients. And…" But I had become tongue-tied.

THE DOCTOR'S BAG

Medicines

In the 1830s, doctors made many medicines themselves. Some were made from local plants; others might be ordered from a chemist. Medicated "dough" was rolled into a long strip and cut into pills. Medicines also came as liquids or as powders wrapped in individually folded papers.

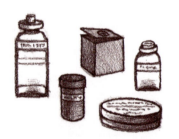

Disturbing News

> ### FIRST WOMAN DOCTOR?
>
> Margaret Anne Bulkley attended medical school in Scotland disguised as a man. She called herself Dr. James Barry, and she kept up her disguise for more than forty years, working all over the world. She ended up in Canada when she was in her sixties. As a British Army medical officer, she was appointed Inspector-General of Hospitals for Upper and Lower Canada (Ontario and Quebec) in 1857, many years before women were licensed to practice medicine in Canada. Her secret only became known after her death.
>
> ---
>
> *When Harriot Hunt attempted to enter medical school in the United States in 1847, she was flatly refused. "We object to having the company of any female forced upon us," the male students announced. They felt she would be sacrificing "her modesty by appearing with men in the lecture room."*

Mama continued for me. "And perhaps those of us who couldn't actually wield a hammer could help in other ways."

"Yes!" Voices boomed out enthusiastically. "A marvelous idea!"

A few shook their heads. "Build it with what?" they said scornfully. But my idea was like a spark that had started a fire blazing.

Hands rose. Someone offered to donate lumber. A member of the parish suggested that the house should be made of stone, similar to the church. He said he would be responsible for hauling the stone from the quarry to the site. Someone else agreed to donate nails, and almost everyone volunteered their time.

"Let's fetch Dr. H. right now!" said the man with the gravely voice, and I was given the honor. A few of the other children came with me.

Somehow I managed to keep a straight face when Dr. Hutchison answered the door.

"You must come," I insisted. "It's an emergency at the new church." Instinctively he reached for his coat and his staff.

"And could you please bring your wife?" one of the other children asked. Dr. H. looked puzzled.

I struggled for the right words. "There is a lady involved, you see." Probably imagining that someone was having a baby, Mrs. H. nodded and quickly threw her shawl around her shoulders. Then her face fell as she looked at her sons. Obviously William, James, John, Henry and George couldn't be left on their own. They would destroy the cottage in no time.

"They can come to our house," said one of the boys in the group. "We live right next to the church."

William walked along beside me. "What's going on?" he asked suspiciously.

"Wait and see!" I said it with a casual shrug, but my heart was pounding.

When they all realized that the crowd had gathered together in the church on their behalf, even the boys were speechless.

"We will build you a house. A house of stone that will stand forever. It will be the finest stone house in Peterborough, and it will have lots of space for your growing family."

"I…I don't know what to say…" Dr. Hutchison's voice was almost a whisper.

"Oh, John!" said his wife. "Just say yes!"

"Yes, Father, say yes," echoed the boys.

Dr. H. smiled at his wife and sons and then at the crowd.

"Yes," he said.

THE MEDICINE GARDEN
Garlic: For curing diarrhea and relieving coughs.

FIVE

The Bonfire House

Just a few days later, I saw buggies and wagons and crowds of people gathering down the road from our house.

"Something is going on," I said to Mama, and I leaned far out on the garden gate trying to see better.

"Surprise!" said Mama. She had a broad smile on her face. "That is Dr. Hutchison's piece of land. That is where the house will be built."

"You mean he's going to be our neighbor?"

She nodded. I was so happy I danced around the garden until I was too puffed to continue.

The project began immediately. When I was supposed to be in bed, I would watch from my window. The workers were all volunteers, so they had to do their work in the evenings when they had finished their daytime jobs. They cut the trees, then stacked the wood and brush in enormous piles around the edge of the property.

Carts arrived full of stone and lumber, and within just a few weeks a house began to grow. Carpenters, joiners, roofers and stonemasons bustled around the site.

Autumn came, and when the days grew shorter and the light faded, the workers lit up the brush piles. Each evening when they arrived, they simply stoked up the fires, added a little more brush to make a big blaze and did their work by firelight.

People carrying lanterns would walk over to watch. The house became known as the Bonfire House.

One evening Mama and I took tea to the workers. She handed out the steaming cups and I followed with a plate of my scones. I stared in wonder at the house. Glass had been fitted into the two front windows, and the new panes reflected the firelight.

"Will you look at that!" said the glazier.

"It's as though the house has eyes!" said a stonemason.

Night after night the Bonfire House did appear to be watching the activity that surrounded it.

When it was time for the painters to do their work, it was frosty cold. They worked quickly, trying to complete their task before the first snow.

Most days, on his way home from his rounds, Dr. Hutchison would stop by. On these visits he often had to patch up one of the workers. Not all the men had built houses before, and there were a number of cuts and bruises.

Two of the accidents were serious. Gavin Macintosh's son slipped on the ice behind a horse that was hauling stone. He was kicked in the chest and broke several ribs. Two days later Graeme Murray fell from the roof when he was carrying shingles. He was unconscious for so long, no one expected he would live. Miraculously, he did wake up, and though he had broken an arm and a leg, the crack to his head left no lasting damage.

THE DOCTOR'S BAG

Plasters and Poultices

Doctors would carry the ingredients for making plasters and poultices. To make a plaster, a healing substance (such as a mustard ointment) would be spread on a cloth bandage that would then stick to the body to protect a wound or help cure an ailment. Poultices were made by applying a warm porridgelike mixture to sores or inflamed parts of the body to soothe or relieve pain.

At last the big day arrived. The Hutchison family moved in and we had a house-warming party. Neighbors and friends came from miles around with roasts, pies, cakes and scones. Fires were lit in all the fireplaces. Candles and lanterns shone from every window.

By now George was an accomplished crawler, and he was just learning to walk and was threatening to fall down the stairs, so I picked him up and we stood back out of harm's way as William, James, John and Henry raced from room to room. They examined the keeping room on the lower level, then thundered back up the stairs and up the ladder to the sleeping loft. George and I wandered more slowly from room to room. I admired all the new up-to-date conveniences, especially the built-in clothes cupboards in the two bedrooms.

THE KEEPING ROOM

A keeping room was far more than a kitchen; it was the family living room. In the keeping room at Hutchison House, Martha Hutchison kept all the food, her baby by the fireside during the day, her wool for spinning, tubs for doing the laundry (and for taking baths), drying racks for the clothes and much more.

There was also a cot or daybed where an older child sometimes slept on a cold winter's night to keep the fire going, where guests could sleep if they were staying over, or where a sick child could spend the day.

When Mama and I left the party, it was dark. The bonfires in the garden had faded to glowing embers. Now all the warmth and light came from inside the house.

❦

With the Hutchisons as neighbors, my days were full. The boys became my good friends, and we visited back and forth almost every day.

When the older boys were busy, I would help Mrs. Hutchison with the younger ones, reading to them or taking them for walks. Best of all, I was occasionally able to help Dr. Hutchison when he needed an extra pair of hands. He often saw patients at home now. I learned how to distract frightened children as they waited in the front hall, and I made tea for their anxious parents.

One afternoon Mama shared some exciting news with me. Mrs. Hutchison was going to have another baby.

"Oh, Mama," I exclaimed. "Maybe this one will be a girl!"

"It would be lovely if it was," she said somewhat sadly, and she told me about the Hutchisons' two daughters who had died when they were infants. Almost every family we knew had lost at least one child. Mama had not lost a child…but we had lost Papa.

THE MEDICINE GARDEN
Raspberry leaf: Raspberry leaf tea has long been used to help prepare women for childbirth, and to relieve morning sickness and menstrual discomfort.

A few months later, on a cold, blustery winter evening, I heard someone on our doorstep. I expected it was Mama, returning from the village. She had been helping poor Mrs. Stevenson whose husband had just died. But the door burst open and it was William, with James, John, Henry and George behind him.

"Quick, Kathleen, fetch your mother! The baby is coming!"

"She's not here. She's with Mrs. Stevenson." I thought quickly. "But I'll go, William. You stay here with the boys and Mama will be back in time to help you bed everybody down for the night."

As I wrapped my shawl around my shoulders, William and I came up with a signal. I would put one candle in the window if the baby was a boy, two if it was a girl.

Dr. H. raised an eyebrow as I explained why I had come instead of Mama. I expect he thought I was too young to even understand where babies came from. But there was no time to dwell on such matters. I was simply put to work.

THE DOCTOR'S BAG
Obstetric Forceps
A large pincerlike instrument used to help deliver babies.

I rubbed Mrs. Hutchison's back for her, braided her long hair and

> ## CHILDBIRTH
>
> In the 1800s women generally had their babies at home. Women helped each other when a baby was due. One neighbor would look after the older children, often taking them home with her for a few days. Another would make the mother-to-be comfortable, boil water and prepare the cradle by the fireside. Another neighbor would alert the doctor or midwife — a woman trained or experienced in helping other women give birth.
>
> Midwives have attended births throughout recorded history, and in Dr. Hutchison's day it was far more common to have a midwife in attendance than a doctor. As medical schools increased in number, midwifery became less popular. However, in recent years midwives have regained their status. Today in North America, midwives are certified professionals who deliver babies both in private homes and in hospitals.

washed her face with a warm cloth. Time flew, and so did I — up and down the stairs, building up fires, boiling water, warming small sheets and blankets by the fire and finding instruments for Dr. H. in his office.

Then Dr. H. suddenly shooed me off to make raspberry leaf tea. I wanted to explain to him that I should stay, because I was going to be a doctor. But he was firm, and I could tell this was no time for discussion.

I was in the keeping room making the tea when I heard the first lusty cry.

"A boy, Martha. Another bonnie, healthy boy," Dr. Hutchison said.

I have to admit my heart sank a little as I placed one candle in the window, but the Hutchisons didn't seem to be the least bit sad. I understood why when I took them the tea and saw the baby. He was beautiful!

"What will you call him?" I asked.

"We'll christen him Ralph Burton Hutchison," said his proud mama. "But we'll call him Burton. You'll be able to take him for walks when he's a little older."

"Yes," said Dr. H. "We can't trust our scalawag boys with Burton, but we can certainly trust you, Kathleen."

THE MEDICINE GARDEN
Sage: Tea made from the leaves was used as a remedy for coughs, colds, constipation, liver complaints and rheumatic pain.

It was late when I left the Bonfire House. The night was cold and crystal clear. I was exhausted, but I was far too excited to think of sleep.

I stretched my arms up to the sky, feeling as though I could touch the stars. I picked the brightest one I could see and almost shouted my wish: *Star light, star bright, first star I see tonight, I wish I may, I wish I might…be a doctor some day, just like Dr. Hutchison.*

Before going inside, I glanced back. The Bonfire House was still watching! One winking, twinkling eye, my telltale candle, sent a warm, luminous glow across the snow.

EPILOGUE

The Hutchisons did eventually have a daughter who survived childbirth. In fact, they had three girls. Sarah, the first, died before her fourth birthday — three days before her sister Frances Mary came into the world. A year later, in 1844, Mary Elizabeth was born, and the Hutchison family was complete.

In 1847, hundreds of desperately sick Irish immigrants arrived in Peterborough. En route to Canada they had become ill with typhus, a highly infectious and often fatal disease. Isolation shelters were constructed for them on the outskirts of town, and Dr. H. offered his assistance without hesitation. But he was already tired and run down, and within days he became sick himself. Close contact was dangerous, and no neighbors or friends dared to go near the house. His wife, Martha, nursed him, assisted only by her sister-in-law who had been staying with the family.

John Hutchison died within a week, at the age of fifty. The two women quickly prepared his body for immediate burial. No other member of the Hutchison family contracted the disease. Ten thousand of the eighty-five thousand settlers who arrived in Canada in 1847 died during that epidemic. Thirty thousand more became seriously ill.

Not long after Dr. Hutchison's death, the Bonfire House was sold. The family moved to Toronto, where they had relatives. In 1969, the house was generously bequeathed to the Peterborough Historical

Society by Mrs. Connal Brown. Her family had owned the house for more than one hundred years. It was decided that it should be restored as a museum, and that it should be called Hutchison House.

The house was old by this time and in need of a great deal of repair. The citizens of Peterborough knew its history and felt it was worth saving. Once again they worked together. They set up a fundraising campaign with the slogan "Built by the Citizens, Restored by the Citizens." As in 1836, donations were made: wood for the fireplaces, new flooring, volunteer hours and funding.

In the Hutchison House Museum, one can imagine Dr. Hutchison sitting at his office desk or having a quiet cup of tea in the parlor. There is still the sound of children's footsteps in the hall and the sound of laughter echoing up the stairs from the keeping room. Many of the visitors are children and, like Kathleen, they are drawn by the warmth and magic of the Bonfire House.

GLOSSARY

Anesthetic A drug or gas used by a doctor to put a patient to sleep or induce numbness and remove pain.

Bacteria Germs; microscopic organisms living in soil, air and water that can cause disease.

Cholera A severe infectious disease of the intestines, frequently epidemic and often causing death.

Convalescence A period of rest when a patient regains strength and health after a serious illness or injury.

Corduroy road A road laid crosswise with logs to cover wet, marshy areas, usually resulting in an extremely bumpy surface similar to the ridges on corduroy material.

Coroner An official who investigates a death suspected of occurring from other than natural causes.

Epidemic A rapidly spreading outbreak of a severe disease, affecting many people at the same time.

Flint A hard stone that makes a spark when struck against steel.

Forceps An instrument that functions like a pair of pincers.

Galloping consumption A form of consumption (tuberculosis/lung disease) that progresses at an unusually rapid rate.

Gangrene A severe bacterial infection in the tissues surrounding a wound, which results in lack of blood circulation and causes the tissue to die.

Glazier A craftsperson who provides a house with windows and sets the glass in place.

Joiner A skilled carpenter who usually works on the interior finishing details of a house.

Justice of the peace A person permitted to grant licenses, perform marriages and try minor cases.

Lancet A surgical instrument used to make incisions.

Obstetrics The branch of medicine that deals with pregnancy and childbirth.

Opium A drug that is used in medicines for its pain-killing, sleep-inducing properties, but is dangerous and habit-forming.

Sanitarium (Sanatorium) An establishment for medical treatment and convalescence of patients suffering from tuberculosis and some other diseases.

Scalawag A rascal; a mischievous child.

Sterilize To boil or steam objects to free them from bacteria; to disinfect, purify.

Typhoid fever An infectious disease that causes intestinal inflammation, spread by contaminated food or water and often fatal.

Typhus A highly infectious disease that causes fever, extreme headache, purple spots on the skin and delirium. Spread by lice and fleas.

Vaccine A medicinal solution prepared and given by injection (vaccination) to help prevent disease.

FOR FURTHER INFORMATION

Read more about medicine in the 1800s:

Cochrane, Jennifer, *An Illustrated History of Medicine*, Tiger Books International, 1996.

Jennings, Gael (illustrations by Roland Harvey), *Bloody Moments: Highlights from the Astonishing History of Medicine*, Annick, 2000.

Johnstone, Michael, *Medicine News*, Candlewick Press, 2000.

Parker, Steve, *Medicine*, Stoddart, 1995.

Storring, Rod, *A Doctor's Life: A Visual History of Doctors and Nurses Through the Ages*, Dutton, 1998.

Ward, Brian, *The Story of Medicine*, Lorenz Books/Anness Publishing, 2000.

Read more about Margaret Anne Bulkley/Dr. James Barry:

Town, Florida, *A Silent Companion*, Red Deer College Press, 1999.

Read more about life in the 1800s:

Brandis, Marianne, *Rebellion: A Novel of Upper Canada*, The Porcupine's Quill, 1996.

Greenwood, Barbara, *A Pioneer Story*, Kids Can Press, 1994. (U.S. edition: *A Pioneer Sampler*)

Parry, Caroline, *Eleanora's Diary: The Journals of a Canadian Pioneer Girl*, Scholastic, 1994.

Learn more about nineteeth-century life and medicine on these Websites (Websites may change without notice. At press time, all sites listed here were in full operation):

http://www.civilization.ca/odyssey.html The Canadian Museum of Civilization. Explore meaningful moments in Canada's history. Tell your own story about a historic object that is special to you.

http://americanhistory.si.edu/ The Smithsonian National Museum of American History. Click onto the "Not Just for Kids" page. Become a historian and follow clues to find out all sorts of details about one nineteenth-century family.

http://www.mtn.org/~quack/ The museum of questionable medical devices!

http://susan.chin.gc.ca/LearnVmc/English/index.html A treasure hunt; a journey of discovery; a new way to find educational materials online.

http://www.heritagefdn.on.ca/Links/linkskids.htm The Ontario Heritage Foundation. Follow the links to pages such as "History Through the Eyes of Those Who Live It" and "Where History Lives on the Net."

http://www.medicalantiques.com/ and
http://www.collectmedicalantiques.com/collection.html Examine a large pink leech jar, long-ago lancets of all shapes and sizes and much more.